THE THREE LITTLE PIGS

THE THREE LITTLE PIGS

Caroline Bucknall

Dial Books for Young Readers · New York

To Kate and Angela

First published in the United States 1987 by
Dial Books for Young Readers
2 Park Avenue
New York, New York 10016
Published in Great Britain by Macmillan Publishers Ltd.
Copyright © 1986 by Caroline Bucknall
All rights reserved
Printed in Hong Kong
First Edition
US
1 3 5 7 9 10 8 6 4 2

Library of Congress Cataloging in Publication Data
Bucknall, Caroline. The three little pigs.
Summary: A retelling in rhyme of the traditional nursery tale,
in which three pigs eventually escape from a hungry wolf.
[1. Folklore. 2. Pigs—Folklore. 3. Stories in rhyme.]
I. Title.
PZ8.3.B849Th 1987   398.2'4529734   [E]   86-16716
ISBN 0-8037-0100-4

The full-color artwork was prepared using black ink
and colored pencils. It was then color-separated
and reproduced as red, blue, yellow, and black halftones.

A rainy day.

The piglets three
were cold and wet beneath a tree.
"We hate the rain. We hate the snow.
Where can we live? Where can we go?"

"I'll build a house," the first pig cried,
"and when it rains, I'll stay inside!"
"A great idea," the others said,
"and when it snows, we'll stay in bed!"

"I'll build a house of straw and hay –
it won't take long, then I can play."

"A house of hay and straw's no good.
I'm building my house out of wood."

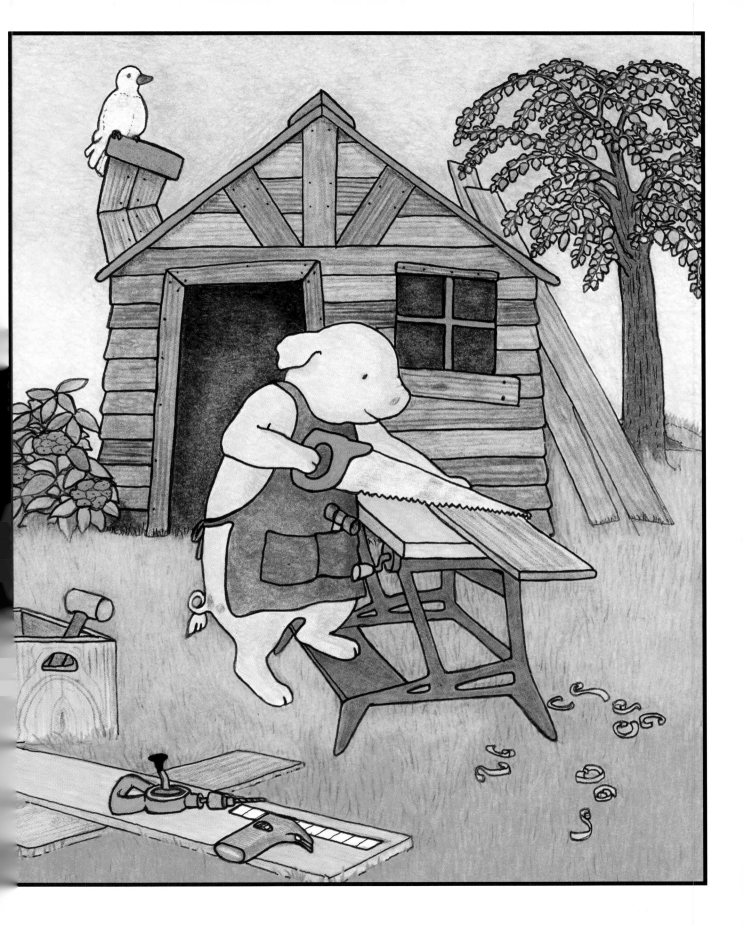

"To build a house of brick takes longer,
but my new home will be much stronger."

"Why work so hard? Why build so strong?"
"The big bad wolf might come along."
"Ha ha! That wolf's no threat," they cried;
"we have new homes, we'll run and hide."

No sooner had they spoken than the wolf appeared.

The piggies ran.

The first pig reached her house of straw.
The wolf soon pounded on the door.
"Oh, tasty pig, come out and meet me!"
"No, never!" cried the pig. "You'll eat me!"

He HUFFED. He PUFFED. The awful blast
blew down the house! The pig was fast.

She reached the wooden house and cried,
"The wolf is here, let me inside!"

The second pig said, "Never fear!
We're safe and sound while we're in here."

The wolf arrived. "Aha," he growled.
"Come out!" "No, never!" both pigs howled.
He HUFFED. He PUFFED. The flimsy shed
was blown apart. The piglets fled.

"The wolf is getting closer to us!
Help!" cried the pigs. "He wants to chew us!"

The third pig heard them. "Come in quick!
You're safe – this house is built of brick."

"He'll huff and puff but here we stay.
He'll never blow this house away."

The wolf HUFF PUFFED with all his might.
The house stood firm. The pigs sat tight.

"No problem. I can reach my snack
by jumping down this chimney stack."

He leapt – and landed in a pot
of boiling water, scalding hot.
When they saw the wolf they feared
was stewed, the little piglets cheered.

The pigs lived happily together . . .

while the big bad wolf endured the weather.